The
SHARK
Who Bit Things
He Shouldn't

Denis Bond

Illustrated by
Valeria Petrone

Coach
House

Look out for more great titles
by Denis Bond and Valeria Petrone

The Dragon Who Couldn't Help Breathing Fire
The Granny Who Wasn't Like Other Grannies
The Monster Who Couldn't Scare Anyone
The Train Who Was Frightened Of the Dark
The Witch Who Loved To Make Children Cry

Further copies of this book or other books in the series are
available from Coach House Publications Ltd

You can also order online from
www.coachhouseonline.co.uk

Coach House Publications Ltd
The Coach House,
School Green Road,
Freshwater,
Isle of Wight
PO40 9BB

First published in the UK in 1998 by
Scholastic Children's Books

This edition published in 2004 by
Coach House Publications Ltd

Text copyright © Denis Bond 1998
Illustrations copyright © Valeria Petrone 1998

ISBN 1-899-392-300

Printed in the UK

Down at the bottom of the ocean, among the seaweed and the coral there lived a shark. He was a fearsome shark. He always bit things he shouldn't.

Every morning, as soon as he woke up, he headed straight for the old wrecked ship. He SWISHED across its barnacle-covered deck and swam past its splintered masts, until he came to the large brass cannon.

Here he stared at his reflection and smiled. Then he gazed, lovingly, at his sharp, gleaming white teeth. You're a handsome shark, he thought. Your teeth are so beautiful. So sharp. So white. Perfect for biting things they shouldn't.

None of the other fish in the sea thought that the shark was handsome. And they all thought his teeth were scary. But luckily, because the teeth were so white, they could all see him coming for miles. "SHARK!" they glugged, as they sped away to hide.

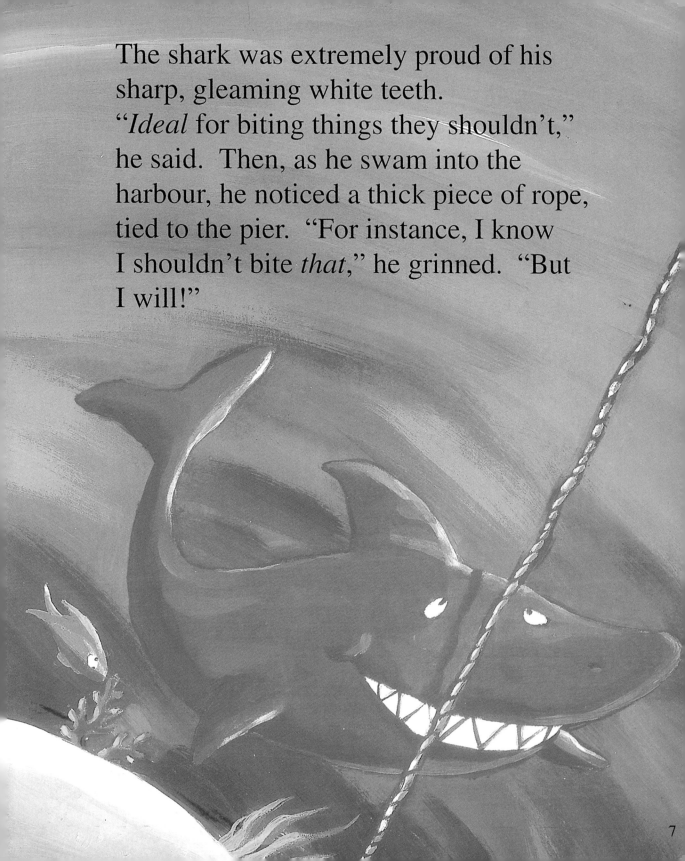

The shark was extremely proud of his
sharp, gleaming white teeth.
"*Ideal* for biting things they shouldn't,"
he said. Then, as he swam into the
harbour, he noticed a thick piece of rope,
tied to the pier. "For instance, I know
I shouldn't bite *that*," he grinned. "But
I will!"

SNAP! went his gleaming white teeth.
SNAP! SNAP! GRIND!
And he bit right through the piece
of rope. A man's angry face, peering
down into the water, suddenly startled
the shark.
"Oi!" the man glugged. He would've
said more than that . . . if he could.
But he couldn't.
"Oi!" GLUG! he went. "Oi!" GLUG!

The other end of the rope was tied to the man's sailing boat . . . and now the man and his boat were slowly drifting out to sea.
As the shark popped his head up from the water and smiled, the man shook his fist furiously.

"I know I shouldn't have bitten that rope," said the shark. "But I *did*!" And he swam on towards the shallow water at the edge of the beach, where there were lots of people paddling in the sea. None of them saw the shark's fin. And none of them saw the gleaming white teeth.

The shark saw two small girls playing
with a beach ball.
"I shouldn't bite *that*," he said. "But I
will!" And he *did*.

Then he saw a little boy with a shrimping
net on the end of a thin wooden cane.
"And I shouldn't bite that," he said.
"But I will!"
And he *did*.

Then the shark got terribly excited! He
noticed three small children floating
towards him in a rubber dinghy.
"I know I shouldn't bite *that*!" he said.
"But I will!"
The lifeguard had seen the shark's fin . . .
and he'd seen the shark's gleaming
white teeth.
"SHARK!" he yelled, as he ran into
the water.

But he was too late.
SNAP! went the gleaming white teeth.
SNAP! SNAP! GRIND!
BANG! went the rubber dinghy.
BANG! Hisssss!
The terrified children tumbled into
the water, where the lifeguard quickly
saved them.

One man was still paddling. He hadn't
heard the cry of "SHARK!" He was
bending over, picking up pretty shells
from the sea-bed.
I know I shouldn't, thought the shark.
But I will!
SNAP! he went on the man's bottom.
He didn't bite too hard. And he didn't
go, SNAP! SNAP! GRIND! He gave
just one tiny nip!
The man yelped and leapt into the air.
"SHARK!" he shrieked.

That afternoon, lots of people had gathered on the town hall steps to see the mayor.

"Stop the shark! Stop the shark!" they yelled.

"You must do something!" complained a man who was holding some pretty shells in one hand and rubbing his bottom with the other.

The mayor went to the aquarium where the aquarium owner showed him around. There were tanks of brightly coloured fish and sea horses and eels.
"I see you haven't got a shark, though," said the mayor. "Would you like one?" The aquarium owner leapt up and down with joy. "Ooh, yes please!" he said.

So the mayor sent out a helicopter to
search for the shark . . . and as it circled
above the sea, the pilot used his
binoculars, trying to catch sight of the
fearsome creature with the sharp,
gleaming white teeth. But he couldn't
see it anywhere.

The mayor also sent out a fishing boat
with a large net. The captain instructed
his crew to look out for something bright
and shiny in the water. "That'll be its
teeth," he explained.
The boat travelled for miles and miles
looking for the shark. But it was
nowhere to be seen.

As the helicopter and the boat disappeared into the distance, a granny arrived on the end of the pier, holding a rod. She wanted to do some fishing. "What are we going to use for bait?" her grandson asked her. "We'll need to use a maggot, or a worm, or a piece of bread." "How about your toffee-apple?" suggested Granny.

The shark was basking beneath the pier and when he saw a toffee-apple on a piece of string plop into the water, right in front of his eyes, he couldn't believe his luck.

"I know I shouldn't," he said. "But I will!"

"If we're lucky we might catch a kipper for tea, Granny," said her grandson.
"We may even catch some fish fingers."
Granny laughed. "Perhaps we'll catch the shark!" she joked.
She suddenly stopped laughing when she felt a sharp tug on her fishing line.
It almost pulled her into the water.

The shark realised immediately that he shouldn't have bitten into the toffee-apple. It had got stuck to his sharp, gleaming white teeth. He couldn't open his mouth properly. He couldn't go SNAP! And he certainly couldn't go SNAP! SNAP! GRIND!
He pulled and pulled at the fishing line.

Granny's grandson leaned over the edge of the pier. He could see a fin. And he could see something bright and shiny under the water.

"SHARK!" he shouted.

And "SHARK!" yelled Granny.

People came rushing along the pier to see what was happening.

"Help me!" cried Granny. "I'm being pulled over the edge."
Her grandson quickly wrapped his arms around her waist. An old man held on to the grandson. And a police officer held on to the old man.
They pulled and pulled and pulled.
And the fishing rod began to bend.

Very soon, there was a trail of people
stretching right along the pier. They
were all holding on to each other.
And they were pulling at the fishing line
which was attached to the toffee-apple . . .
which was stuck to the shark's gleaming
white teeth.

"Yes!" yelled Granny excitedly, as she suddenly managed to pull her fishing line out of the water.

"Got him!" she screeched.

"Hooray!" everyone yelled, as they tumbled backwards, landing heavily on each other.

"Granny's caught the shark!"

But Granny hadn't caught the shark!
On the end of her fishing line was the
toffee-apple. And stuck to the
toffee-apple were the shark's sharp,
gleaming white teeth.
Everyone stared and pointed at the teeth.
Then they all laughed and laughed.

But Granny didn't laugh. She felt sorry
for the shark. And when he popped his
head out of the water and she saw how
embarrassed he looked . . . and she saw
the tears in his eyes, she understood
exactly how he felt.

"Mine do that sometimes," she said.
"Look!"
And she took out her own teeth and
waved them at the shark.
The shark smiled . . . and Granny smiled.
They were both wide, gummy kind of
smiles.

Granny quickly removed the sticky toffee-apple from the shark's teeth and handed them back to him. And as he swam away, feeling happy again, Granny called after him.

"Use them for eating," she said. "And use them for smiling," she added. "Don't use them to bite things you shouldn't."

Later that week, the shark saw something
very interesting floating on the water.
It was a li-lo. And on the li-lo were two
people; peacefully, happily sunbathing.
The shark swam closer. "Now, I know
I shouldn't bite that," he said.
And he didn't!